The Caterpillar Woman

INHABIT
MEDIA

Published by Inhabit Media Inc.
www.inhabitmedia.com

Inhabit Media Inc. (Iqaluit) P.O. Box 11125, Iqaluit, Nunavut, X0A 1H0
(Toronto) 191 Eglinton East, Suite 301, Toronto, M4P 1K1

Edited by Louise Flaherty and Kelly Ward
Art direction by Danny Christopher

This project was made possible in part by the Government of Canada.

We acknowledge the support of the Canada Council for the Arts for our publishing program.

Printed in Canada.

Library and Archives Canada Cataloguing in Publication

Sammurtok, Nadia, author
     The caterpillar woman / by Nadia Sammurtok ; illustrated
by Carolyn Gan.

ISBN 978-1-77227-083-9 (hardback)

     I. Gan, Carolyn, illustrator II. Title.

PS8637.A5384C37 2016   jC813'.6   C2016-903224-8

The Caterpillar Woman

By Nadia Sammurtok • Illustrated by Carolyn Gan

Piujuq was a beautiful young woman. She enjoyed spending time alone at her favourite lake close to her camp. She loved to dance alone with the butterflies by the lake, imagining beautiful rhythms in her head.

This was when Piujuq felt most at peace.

One day, Piujuq decided to take a walk to the lake. During her walk, Piujuq noticed a figure up ahead. This figure was walking towards her. Piujuq was curious, because she did not usually cross paths with anyone on this walk.

As the figure got closer, she realized it was a woman. This woman appeared to have skin unlike Piujuq's. It sort of glowed, and had a tinge of green to it. It reminded Piujuq of the skin of an insect.

Eventually, Piujuq met the strange woman. The woman spoke first, introducing herself as Tarraq. Tarraq told Piujuq that she had gotten lost and was trying to find her camp.

"I am so cold," Tarraq said as she shivered. "I have been walking for a long time and I only have this thin jacket to wear. Would you be willing to give me your parka?" Tarraq asked.

Piujuq wasn't sure at first if she should trade parkas with a stranger. Tarraq's jacket looked very thin, and it was made from skins that Piujuq had never seen before. But Piujuq eventually agreed because she did not want Tarraq to be cold. Piujuq was a kind young woman, and was known in her camp for being very giving and helpful to others. Piujuq felt sorry for Tarraq, so she agreed and gave Tarraq her warm clothing.

Piujuq and Tarraq went their separate ways. Soon after, Piujuq began to feel chilly, so she put on the coat that Tarraq had left her with. As soon as Piujuq pulled on the coat, an odd feeling came over her. She looked at her hands and realized that her skin was changing.

Piujuq's skin began to transform from a smooth, beautiful tanned colour to a prickly, fuzzy, green colour. She was afraid of what was happening to her, and she did not know whether she should go home to her camp or not, so she continued to walk on to her favourite lake.

When she arrived at the lake, Piujuq looked at her reflection in the water. What she saw terrified her. Not only did she have prickly, fuzzy, green skin, but her face and her hair were horrible. She had long, green, spiny hair growing out in every direction. She no longer looked like herself.

It was then that Piujuq realized that the jacket the stranger had given her had turned her into a caterpillar. She decided that it was best that she not return home to her camp, as she did not want to frighten her family.

Piujuq began to wander the land, lost and afraid. Eventually she found an abandoned tent and stayed there. She lived alone for many months, having no contact with anyone.

Then, one day, as Piujuq lay in her tent, sad and alone, she heard the old familiar sounds of people travelling. She could hear Inuit laughing and talking, and the sound of their *kamiit* crunching against the dry tundra. Piujuq excitedly peeked out of her tent and saw a group of three men walking towards her.

The men saw the tent and entered it. They appeared confused and curious as to who she was. Piujuq offered them tea, and, having noticed the rips in their clothing, offered to mend the holes. While mending their clothing, Piujuq told them who she was and where she came from. She told them about her meeting with the strange woman, and that she had once lived with her family but was now afraid of frightening them with her appearance, so she chose to live alone in her tent.

Piujuq later learned that the men were on a journey to find themselves wives. A part of her was hopeful that one of them would take her as his wife, but none of them offered. This made her feel sad, because she knew that the reason they did not want her was because she looked like a caterpillar, and not like a regular woman.

Once Piujuq had finished mending the men's clothing, they left and continued on with their journey. Piujuq was again alone. She stared at her hands, which shared the same kind of skin as the caterpillar crawling on the floor next to her. She began to cry.

Then, suddenly, Piujuq was startled by the sound of something moving outside her tent. She looked outside and saw that one of the men had returned.

Piujuq asked the man, "Why are you here? You better hurry or you will lose the others."

The man introduced himself as Amaruq and replied, "You are very kind. I would like to have you as my wife."

Piujuq was surprised and could not speak. She did not expect that any of these men, or any others for that matter, would look past her physical appearance, but it seemed that this man had.

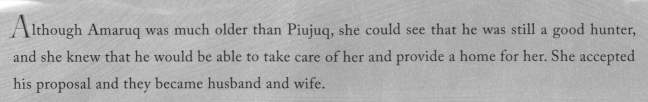

Although Amaruq was much older than Piujuq, she could see that he was still a good hunter, and she knew that he would be able to take care of her and provide a home for her. She accepted his proposal and they became husband and wife.

Piujuq and her new husband fell in love, and as each new day passed, their love for each other grew. Amaruq took great care of his wife, and she of him. One day, as they were sharing stories, Piujuq told Amaruq that before she became a caterpillar she had loved to dance. After talking about her love of music, Piujuq asked Amaruq if he would make her a drum, so she could dance once again. He agreed, and told her that he would make her the most beautiful drum she had ever seen.

The next day, Amaruq set out to search for materials for the drum he had promised to make for his wife. As he was walking, he came across a small cave close to a shoreline that was often flooded at high tide. He thought this would be the perfect place to find some driftwood that could be used to make a drumbeater.

Although dark, and deep enough that no sunlight reached inside, the walls of the cave appeared to shimmer, as if by magic. To his surprise, Amaruq came across a drumbeater, already complete, laying on the cave floor. Amaruq was ecstatic.

Although the beater appeared to be old, it was still very beautiful. Amaruq felt that it was pretty enough to give to his wife. He assumed it had been abandoned, and so he happily picked it up and began his journey back home, where his wife awaited his arrival.

As soon as Amaruq returned home, he began working on the drum. He worked on it for many days. He wanted to make Piujuq happy, so he worked very hard on this drum. Once Amaruq was finished with the drum, and was pleased with its appearance, he showed it to Piujuq. As soon as she held it in her hands, Piujuq felt something come over her. It was a feeling of happiness that she couldn't describe, but one she knew she hadn't felt in the years since becoming a caterpillar.

Piujuq asked Amaruq to play for her. And so, he played while she danced.

As she danced, she began to feel lighter. She looked at her hands and noticed the fuzzy, prickly, green skin beginning to shed! She looked over at her husband and was amazed to see that he too was beginning to change. As he happily beat the drum, he slowly became young again, while she was becoming beautiful again with each step of her dance.

As Amaruq continued to play the drum, Piujuq danced. She danced until she could not dance any longer. When they were finished, Piujuq and Amaruq looked at each other.

Amaruq, who had fallen in love with this not very beautiful, yet very kind, woman was lost for words as he stared at his now beautiful wife. Piujuq, who had fallen in love with the old stranger who took such great care of her, saw a man who suddenly appeared young and strong.

Amaruq looked down at the drum and beater in his hands. He wondered whether there had been some kind of power in the music. Or in the old drumbeater he'd found in that cave.

What Piujuq and Amaruq did not know was that the drumbeater that Amaruq had taken home from the mysterious cave did carry a special type of power. It had been left behind by their ancestors, thousands of years before, in that abandoned cave, and it still carried some of the magic that existed when the world was new.

Because Piujuq had a good, kind heart, she became beautiful, like she once had been. And Amaruq, who was becoming old and weak before finding the wooden beater, became young and strong again because he had the kindness in his heart to see Piujuq's beauty, despite her outward appearance. They were rewarded for their kindness and the unconditional love they had for each other.

And so, Piujuq, who was once a caterpillar, lived the rest of her days beautiful once more.

She felt like the butterflies she once danced with by her favourite lake, freed from her cocoon.

Contributors

Nadia Sammurtok is an Inuit writer and educator originally from Rankin Inlet, Nunavut. Nadia is passionate about preserving the traditional Inuit lifestyle and Inuktitut language so that they may be enjoyed by future generations. Nadia currently lives in Iqaluit, Nunavut, with her son.

Caroyln Gan is an illustrator and designer working in Sydney, Australia. She has worked in television as a visual development artist, colour stylist, and set designer. *The Caterpillar Woman* is her first book.

Inuktitut Pronunciation Guide

In Inuktitut, sometimes the letters *r* and *q* are pronounced with a special sound that is made deep in the back of the throat using the back of the tongue and the uvula. These sounds are known as a "deep r" and a "deep q."

Piujuq
Pronounced "pee-oo-yoq" (with a deep q)—Translates as "beautiful."

Tarraq
Pronounced "tah-rr-aq" (with a deep r and a deep q)—Translates as "shadow."

Amaruq
Pronounced "ah-mah-rooq" (with a deep r and a deep q)—Translates as "wolf."

Kamiit
Pronounced "kah-meet"—Inuktitut name for Inuit snow boots.

Iqaluit • Toronto